FGHIJK

QRSTU

ABCDE

LMNOP

D0618446

I love
California
an ABC adventure
Sandra Magsamen

California is filled with fantastic and beautiful things to see and do. Just follow the **A, B, C's,** there is an amazing adventure waiting for you!

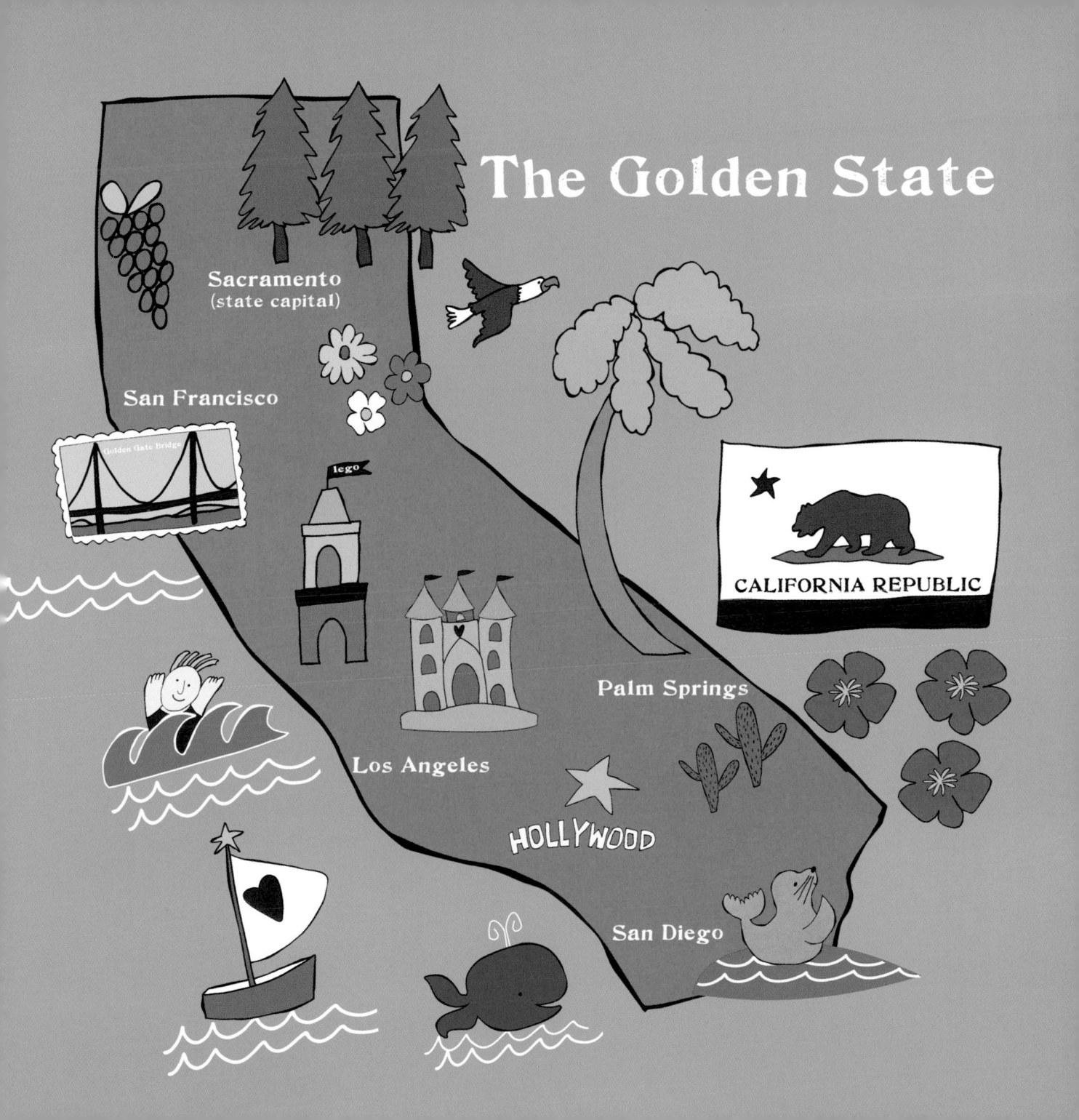
The Golden State
Sacramento
(state capital)
San Francisco
Golden Gate Bridge
Iego
CALIFORNIA REPUBLIC
Palm Springs
Los Angeles
HOLLYWOOD
San Diego

A is for
awesome
because that's
what California is
in every way!

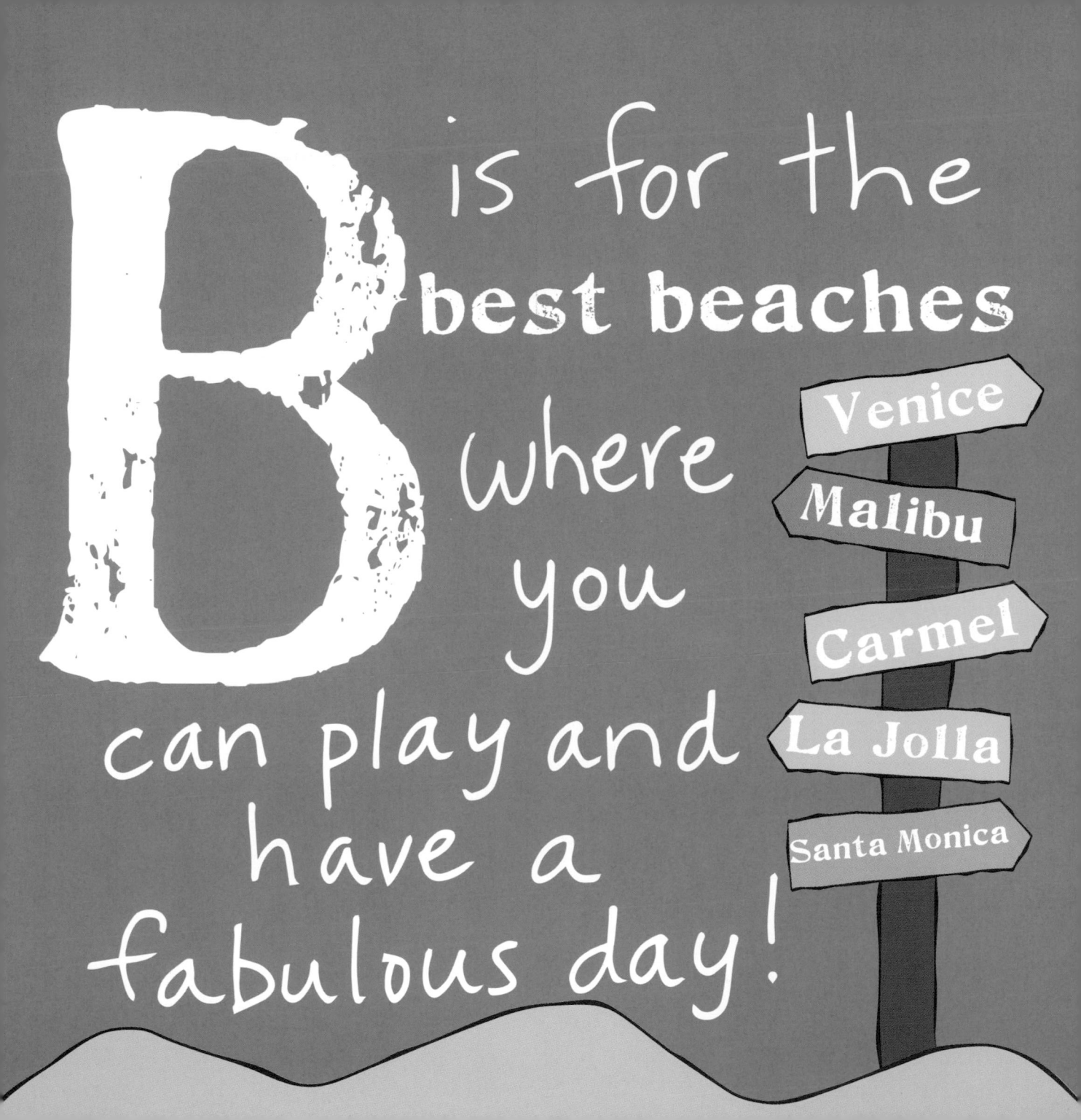
B is for the
best beaches
where
you
can play and
have a
fabulous day!
Venice
Malibu
Carmel
La Jolla
Santa Monica

C is for
cool
trees
like
the sequoia
and redwood.

D is for
Disneyland.
Haven't
been yet?
You should!

E is for
the bald
eagles
found
soaring through the sky
at Joshua Tree.

F is for the wild flowers

from the Sierra Nevada to the sea.

G is for the **Golden Gate Bridge,**

one of our most favorite things.

H is for
Hollywood,
where actors
play chiefs,
cowgirls and kings.
HOLLYWOOD

I is for
what the
incredible
Monterey Bay
aquarium can teach.

J is for
jumping
through all
the big, tall,
cool, gnarly
waves at
Laguna
Beach.

K is for the
kites
flown
in
Santa Barbara above
the sand.

L is for a great day spent at the fantastic **Legoland.**

M is for the
monarch
butterflies
that magically flutter
and fill the air.

N is for
nuts,
like sweet
almonds and
pistachios,
that grow
everywhere.

O is for
Oakland
A's
baseball
on a
hot
summer day.
Athletics

P is for the
Pacific
Ocean
where we all
can play.
Eureka !

Q is for quietly gazing at the stars that shine bright.
napa

R is for the Rose Parade, fun from morning to night.
we love Pasadena

S is for
sailing
off
Catalina on
a windy
day.

T is for
a trip
to
Palm Springs
to see a green
cactus sway.

U is for unicorns.
the golden state
In California magic and wonder are always made.

V is for the **violins** at the Los Angeles Philharmonic being played.

W is for
whale
watching
at Newport
Beach, an
experience
to share.

X is for the
XOXO
Californians love to
spread everywhere.

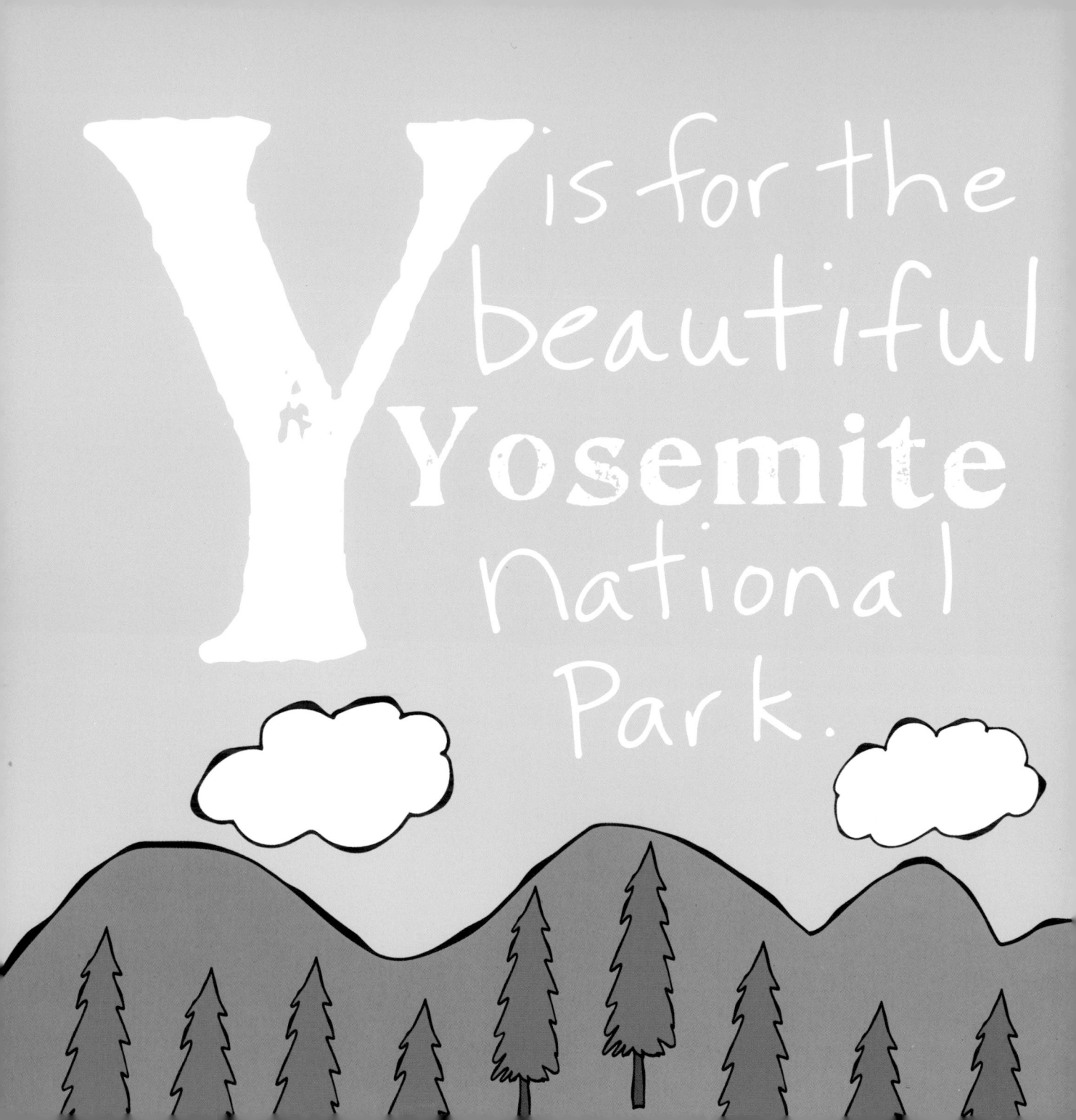
Y is for the
beautiful
Yosemite
National
Park.

Z is for the
ZOO
where grey
sea lions
swim around
and
bark.
San Diego
Zoo

And now our big
has come to
but you
back to
begin

adventure
an end,
can go
A and
again!
lego
San Diego
Zoo

Sandra Magsamen is a best-selling and award-winning artist, author, and designer whose meaningful and message-driven art has touched millions of lives, one heart at a time. She loves to travel and has had many awesome adventures around the world. For now, she lives happily and artfully in Vermont with her family and their dog, Olive.

A big thank you to my amazing studio team of Hannah Barry and Karen Botti. Their creativity, research tenacity and spirit of adventure have been invaluable as we crafted the ABC adventure series.

Sandra Magsamen

Text and illustrations © 2015 Hanny Girl Productions, Inc. www.sandramagsamen.com
Exclusively represented by Mixed Media Group, Inc. NY, NY.
Cover and internal design © 2015 by Sandra Magsamen

Sourcebooks and the colophon are registered trademarks of Sourcebooks, Inc.

All rights reserved. No part of this book may be reproduced in any form or by any electronic or mechanical means including information storage and retrieval systems—except in the case of brief quotations embodied in critical articles or reviews—without permission in writing from its publisher, Sourcebooks, Inc.

Published by Sourcebooks Jabberwocky, an imprint of Sourcebooks, Inc.
P.O. Box 4410, Naperville, Illinois 60567-4410
(630) 961-3900
Fax: (630) 961-2168
www.sourcebooks.com

Library of Congress Cataloging-in-Publication data is on file with the publisher.

Source of Production: Leo Paper, Heshan City, Guangdong Province, China
Date of Production: July 2015
Run Number: 5004063

Printed and bound in China.
LEO 10 9 8 7 6 5 4 3 2 1

The Golden State
Sacramento
(state capital)
San Francisco
Golden Gate Bridge
Iego
CALIFORNIA REPUBLIC
Palm Springs
Los Angeles
HOLLYWOOD
San Diego

ABCDE

LMNOP

VWXYZ

FGHIJK